FINANCIAL THRILLER

THE DEAD BANK DIARY

SERIES

I0537600

FOR THOSE IN THE

SHADE

By Anna Schlegel

BOOK TWO

Translation from Russian

Schlegel Press Association

For Those In The Shade by Anna Schlegel
Book Two of The Dead Bank Diary Series

Published by Schlegel Press Association
Friedrichstr. 123
Berlin, Germany 10117

ISBN: 9780986174957

First Edition: August 2015

Translated by Alla Koshechkina
Consultant Andrew Zubov
Cover photography by Getty Images & Maxim Shirkov /Shutterstock

Also By Anna Schlegel
THE DEAD BANK DIARY SERIES

THE DEAD BANK DIARY

Book One of The Dead Bank Diary Series

THE PRINTS ON THE SNOWS OF YESTERYEAR

Book Three of The Dead Bank Diary Series

SOME DAY I`LL HIT A BANK

Book Four of The Dead Bank Diary Series

THE FROZEN DEBT

Book Five of The Dead Bank Diary Series

MY GOD IS MONEY

Book Six of The Dead Bank Diary Series

Coming Soon

Also By Anna Schlegel

THE SLEEPER SERIES

MONEY CAN`T LIE

Book One of The Sleeper Series

ON MYSELF FOR LITTLE MONEY

Book Two of The Sleeper Series

Coming Soon

CONTENTS

AUTHOR'S NOTE

In these books there are no cops, no killings. There is much about the illegal takeover of banks, and a powerful lot of money. I know how to pump up a bank, and how to bankrupt a bank. I love beautiful gray schemes on the verge of crime. My stories are about fraud in the eyes of a swindler. There are no good guys.

I write about the golden-time bankers, from 1998, when neither the police nor the intelligence services, or any crimes haven't prevent the banks to make money.

These novels are not based on a true story, but you will face this reality in every word.

Anna Schlegel

You may live your whole life without getting to know who you are, and sometimes this is for the better

FOR THOSE IN THE SHADE

It was a bank robbery, however this time the gunmen came not for the cash but for the bank itself, and all that followed happened faster than a domino knockdown.

The bank was bankrupted professionally.

Bad debts of the Third World countries, Cuba, Zimbabwe, Morocco, and The Congo have been returned on the bank's balance sheet. Once, the bank sold the debts to itself, to an offshore company.

Who did this?

The banker finds out the bank in Amsterdam... and has taken it over completely.

ABOUT THE SERIES

These are stories about a man who is not alive anymore. He was a financier, a retired intelligence officer. I had the good luck to arrange a couple of financial frauds. We bumped into each other before the recession, in the flood of shit, together in the dust.

After his death I still had power of attorney.

Of course, Victor knew I wouldn't be able to work on his contacts. I had tried. Now it's funny to think of it. I am, and always have been, a go-between, a rat. Nobody needs middlemen. They get rid of them; they send them to Hell. But I had a white shirt with a necktie, and copies of million-strong contracts for oil, gas, diamonds, and rare-earth metals: light-as-air, rolled fax sheets with lots of zeroes. They made me giddy; they made me drunk. And I ran along with them, and easily foisted them for the middlemen: muddy, middle-aged misters.

When some of the first deals failed, I went into hysterics. I wanted to throw everything in.

Once I had a dream. In my dream, I heard a telephone call,

"Miss Schlegel? We need your signature to extend a contract concluded by Mr..."

I woke up scared; something turned over inside of me. I realized that I was spending my life waiting for such a call. It didn't matter where it caught me.

But there was no going back. Once you've taken a step forward, you realize you can't turn back anymore.

Why did he leave all this to me? I looked the papers over, recalling past years, deals, people, talks: everything from the first meeting to the last minute. And I couldn't find anything for me; because it wasn't for me, actually, for the old me. So I changed. I became a con.

My life was changed. Sometimes it was as convincing and disgusting as a life of a whore. It was as inaccessible as the man who despises you. It was like vomit or sweat from the body from heavy hangover shivers. You wish to run, and there's no place to run to. It's a cold stupor. So it's stupid to look at the smeared corpse on the road, and it's impossible to regain consciousness to look away. This passion nests in the heart, and you don't know what is it.

I have his photo, the last one, taken at Arkhangelskoe hospital. Summer. We're sitting on the edge of a dried-up fountain. He embraces me with one arm, and I'm lost next to him. He is gray-haired and corpulent. He has a mocking look. And behind us there are towering white marble angels.

CHAPTER ONE

MARC

Moscow, July 1999

The night was warm and clear. Ilya was to come the next day and I could not sleep in his absence. I stirred up the burnt charcoal in the fireplace and went to close the door.

Through the dim glass of the door opening from the living room to the terrace, through the reflection of my own sharp and unadorned face, I could see a stranger. The man was standing on the porch. He was a heavy-ass about sixty, big and fat as a wild boar.

"Hello, I'm your neighbor. Marc," he named himself, breathing out his words with the smell of booze.

He looked like a German or of Baltic descent, but had no accent. There was something fishy in his smile, opening a row of small and sharp teeth, with watery, arrogant eyes. I felt confused looking his huge body, bloated face, and inverted, wet lips. I felt ill at ease. Yet this Marc looked quite commonplace, almost as an elderly insurance agent. He seemed invisible, observant, even sleek and loutish at the same time. Such people do exist, – they're grey and unseen, expressionless, – as if nothing has ripened inside, no feelings, no love, no hatred, no greed, no strength... They've got neither good nor evil. But in this one felt long – back over – ripe, as if he had overeaten and thrown up, and was ready to eat more. He was filled up and overflowing. One could see it in his drunken, sweaty countenance, in the grey hair stuck to his forehead, in his manner to stand astride as though he owned the place.

I thought unwillingly, *Oh you're a slut, my dear.*

"Nice to meet you. Anna," I greeted him, opening the door, recollecting having glimpsed him some time before.

"You smell of this house," Marc grinned, as if ascertained all he had to know about me, and changing his tone started speaking in a different, more sober voice. "Someone entered the bank. Let's go. I'll drive. Ilya has just called. He's already started."

Marc cast the travel bag onto the backseat and took to the wheel. We raced off in the car and in a couple of minutes we crossed into Rublyovo Highway, – glaring car lights slowly coming from the opposite direction. He beeped a horn and went to overtake, showering the rear cars with grit spray from under his wheels from the verge.

"Someone entered the bank? And what about security?"

"The security guy handles the drinkers and dopers coming round after a dose to the bank through the main entrance. This was no common robber. He knew how to hook into the camera surveillance and pass over the alarm system. The alarm was on while he was inside. There must've been two of them. Or more than two. What can a security guy do alone? Light me a cigarette."

"So why Ilya wouldn't call some private security?" I inquired, making nothing of it all.

"So he called me."

"Argh..." lighting a cigarette for him I started viewing Marc's face, spongy as slush bread and unconcerned, still getting nothing.

"In the case that the alarm had deployed, the security would have come. But this time, the professionals came to the bank. The security would only scare them away. We'd better know who we are dealing with, and what their goal is. Why would they come to Ilya's bank? What do they want? The bank's got no major accounts. And private depositors are very few," Marc was speaking to himself waiting for no response.

The bank was small. They call this type a small, single 'pocket bank'. Such banks normally have a couple of good clients who dispose of the bank as if it were pocket change, without scruples. It was clear this time it was no pure robbery case. This could not happen. This was not the bank one would try to rob.

"I can tell you for sure the bank is void and empty," I started smoking after Marc. "Ilya wouldn't keep his money in his own bank."

"So how is he making money then?" chuckled Marc, embedding his car between two other rows in a soft, insistent way like a knife into the butter.

"No way. He doesn't give a fuck about his bank. Ilya would only start thinking of his bank when someone starts pulling the bank from under his ass, you know."

"Eh... I see you know Ilya really well."

"So how did that guy break into the bank?" I asked, lighting another cigarette for him.

"Through the first floor window. He made it down from the roof at the point of Ilya's office. That means he knew there were no cameras... There is one outdoor camera only. Then the security guy noticed that someone hooked onto the cameras," Marc drew in on his cigarette, he was calm but his neck turned red over his T-shirt collar. "You know to shoot?"

"Yes. Ilya taught me, over here on the deserted abandoned firing ground."

"Could you shoot at a human?"

"Yes."

"You don't like humans much, do you?" Marc gave a hum.

"I like cats. They don't come asking you for money all the time," I joked away as usual. "So what? There's someone walking around the bank... And do we know exactly where he is?"

"The security guy remained at his post. The security post is clearly visible through the entrance door. If he walks away he may scare them off."

"Then, the man is walking around the bank..."

"There is another alarm system in the vault. In the case he doesn't know to switch it off, we'll clearly know where he's walking... Might any of the bank clients keep something in a deposit box? Or in the safe? What could it be? Or this could be a hacker... Shit. Light me a cigarette."

When we approached the bank, the road took the bridge. From a distance through the trimmed maple tree crowns along the highway I could see the parking in front of the bank, and Ilya's car. He'd parked a block from the bank quarters in a dark back-alley.

17

"We'll go to the bank on the same road," Marc said, shutting off the engine next to a residential building.

Marc and me, together we walked along the embankment past the small restaurant of the old wooden river station. It was gently squawking against the water's ebb, slopping with its rotting barrels. It felt cold at the riverside. The old mansion of the bank behind the wrought iron fence was shimmering white between the maple trees. Their globe-shaped crowns were receding, and their carved leaves had a burnt patina. The wind was tearing them and throwing them under foot, crispy and fragile as glass.

On both sides of the bank there were high-rise office buildings. Behind the bank there was a back yard, fenced with a mesh of frost grape from the old high Stalin-era buildings. Through the fine, knotty vines we could see their flaking walls and zinc-coated waterspouts, shimmering in the dark like organ-pipes at church. On the narrow balconies drying linen hung white. There came the smell of fried potatoes and apples.

Keeping to the deep shadow next to the steel mesh, we approached the fire-escape and climbed to the roof. Next to Ilya's office we could see the first floor window had been cut out. Marc took his mountaineering equipment out of the bag. Descending from the wall, Marc nicked into the window and held out his arm for me. We got into a small room behind Ilya's office. Ilya sometimes stayed there overnight and did not want any cameras in that room, or his office. A door from that room opened to the main filing room, where one could get lost among the shelving units. It was quiet in the corridor. I strained my ears to hear the door rustle, or footsteps in the distance. There was nothing. I felt a breath behind my back. It was the wind stirring the curtain through the broken window, and outside, the chilly darkness of the night time street. I felt the nocturnal rawness.

"Where could he be?" Marc whispered giving me his Beretta that I accepted with my hands chilled all of a sudden. "We've got to know fast who we are dealing with. Let's go to the server room. My gut's telling me."

We went into the corridor and walked to the analyst's office. Entering the roomy office I could not recognize it. It was dark and empty inside like a wood before the rain. Or could that be due to the silence where I was scared to smell a breath?

Finally we saw him though a number of open doors. Through a narrow corridor, the analyst's office was connected to the server room, from which another door opened to the filing room. And that one was ajar. He would have exited through the filing room to Ilya's back-office and left the way he entered, by the roof.

He was a masked gunman, squab and slim, middle-aged judging from his stoop and stony, spread back. The mask was hiding his high cheek-bones. He must have been retired Special Force. Across his chest, the man was holding a stub gun. He was standing with his back to us. He must had finished his work, and made for the filing room. Marc gave me a sign to stay behind the door, but I could still see him.

"Stand where you are. Stick'em up," Marc said in a low voice, aiming his gun to his back.

CHAPTER TWO

ILYA

He held his arms up and lit the room with his lighter. It was a Zippo. His arms were corded. The one that squeezed a Zippo was like a ball of earth full of grass roots.

"I'll fire anyway. The files and the whole building will catch on fire," the gunman's voice was hoarse, as if affected by a cold. "Put your gun down. Fuck, you smell of booze all over the bank," he growled. "And let her put the gun down. Nice perfume, baby... "

Marc put his gun on the floor and nodded at me to put mine down. We remained looking at his back. He was leafing through the filing room with a lighter in his hand. Exiting the filing room door, he cast his Zippo onto a pile of papers.

We put that out fast but that was it. He left as he had entered fast and smooth as a cat.

"Marc, he's got a Ukranian accent."

"And this is no robbery."

"Marc, sorry for asking this stupid thing… But why didn't you fire?"

"'Cause he was wearing aramid, all over him. Had I fired at his hand, he would have had time to respond. The building is old. Everything would have burned down in an instant."

Marc dialed Ilya's cell.

"Ilya, I missed him. Sorry. Call your code head," and, ringing off he turned to me, "I'll find that motherfucker anyway. Let's go."

We returned to Ilya's office.

"How did you meet Ilya?" Marc asked.

"I was doing a favor to a friend of mine who wished to raid Ilya's bank. We kept buying out the bank debt on the cheap. That was a year ago. It was so easy before I met Ilya… "

Ilya was tall, lean, and highbrow, with the sort of manners to be in the public eye. One could not get close to him; he would keep everyone at a distance, or send them flying.

Ilya used to have faultless insight. He would simply reach out and grab his money. The money would flow to him so easily. He seemed to be not so picky. One of my friends said he could strip off just about anyone, be that a church or Feds. It was all the same to him who was standing between him and the money. He had no concept whatsoever. He just he wanted money, reached out and took it from whoever, without looking.

"So what about Ilya?"

"He wasn't even bothered to find out who was there to raid his bank. I was thinking initially he would draw out all his money from the bank to leave it as a dummy. But he did quite the opposite: he pumped it up with cash. Such a bank could not be wedged."

"So what happened to that friend of yours?" Marc inquired.

"Peter decided not to outsource funds any more. So once his credit line opens, we will raid another bank."

"...Raid another bank?"

"This is raiding. Nothing criminal. Neat and pure, Marc."

"Do you want a bank?" Marc asked bluntly.

"I just like living this way," I smiled. "If I've got Ilya, I need no bank. Ilya is more than a bank. But I've got no bank named Ilya. I do no business with Ilya. We just share a bed."

Falling asleep with Ilya, I felt like I owed all the money in the world. But by Monday morning, it all disappeared.

We were so different. He was a solid banker, and I was an ex-Securities trader, a jobless middleman, the waste of the market. There was a huge gap between us. He had his bank, debts and money, expensive suits, and just a different life. I had nothing.

He would not have to stand day and night at the China-town public gardens together with a bunch of other middlemen who also had no office. He didn't have to see the faces of all those middle-aged muddy misters, of different breeds but still all so similar. Or see the people burning inside, like the morning after with a hangover, to gulp down what you've got to say, and still not believe a single word of it.

He wouldn't have to listen to similar conversations and run after the void and swallow it, choking and throwing it up. He wouldn't have to wish for any diamonds or rare-earth elements. He wouldn't get into multi-million deals. He wouldn't need, – as he woke up every morning, – think of borrowing another hundred bucks from someone, and dropping into some investment company office to catch a glimpse which was more of a kick in the pants. While every acned stock-broker just out of his white-shirt eggshell would kick me away like a leper.

The thing was not that I needed to catch onto those multi-million deals I kept thinking of not frittering away into mere cents. No. I could still earn good money as a trader. But that would have been the mere difference between selling and buying rates. A two pennyworth handful of safe, petty cash every day only. There was no more than that.

I didn't want a million at once either. No.

The point was I knew how to make money out of thin air. And I had to make things fast.

A year before the default, this infested air of easy cash would get absorbed into the blood with every intake of breath. It contaminated the whole of the stock market, as if it were epidemic cholera. Everyone was sick, and raving of big money, infecting the others. And everyone kept talking the same and selling the same. And there was no way to escape. This was everywhere, just like the virus. You breathe it in and you catch it, just from casual talks and rustles of the fax paper. And I caught it.

So where could I run away from this? Everyone was selling and buying air, making millions right out of thin air, as if they were flowing across the Moscow airspace. And the air itself was inside-out smelling of the ghostly millions, like the city at noonday heat smells of dust and fuel. It was hanging like the boiling, grey fog above the highway. This air smelled of the city streets, the offices, and the perfumes of the long-legged secritutes… – and my white shirt, when I took it off in the evening coming back from the negotiations. It seemed if you set your face up to this air and breathed it in, you could feel the full odor of those megabucks and their sweet taste on your lips. This was the air of public debt, millions of tons of oil and gold, diamonds and immense off-balance accounts. This was the air of the rotting wreckage of the ruined empire.

One still had to know how to trade out of thin air. One had to trust their gut feeling, and know to how to scent live cash behind the ghostly millions. Those addicted to trading this air got infected, and could never heal again. Today, no one would remember those who knew how to close a mullions-strong deal. Multi-million deals used to fall down one by another. Because there were no middlemen involved. However, such failure wouldn't teach the middlemen a thing. They kept running and running after ghostly millions, just like the soldiers lost in the war for money.

Still I kept breathing in this air, drinking it like vodka till I was drunk, and it sweetly poisoned me, burning into my blood with every intake. I got hooked on this trading in air, just like being on drugs, and till now, I haven't been able to get off it.

One day, I realized I couldn't live without this thin air, suffocating and suffering from the thirst for ghostly millions. How could others breathe it and not getting drunk from it? Why would they still have that sober and provident outlook?

Believe it or not, it was a long time before I thought of anything real-life. I just could not think of anything real-life. Any kind of reality, real petty cash, pettiness and heresy of each, and every day, could smash me like a frog against the road. One would think, what's the matter with me? All those other people somehow keep living and working, and none of them died. That is because they had never tasted that big money. They had never been sick for that air like the people who long for a glass of vodka in a hospital. They would not wake up with a sudden feeling, with that taste in their mouth.

It was silly to keep chasing for the ghostly millions, but I had no other way. It had been all cut off. And I remained there running without looking back or thinking of anything else. Not thinking of my aged boots, or my mother's water supply maintenance issue… – Not thinking of what I am per se, without all those multi-million talks.

Very few of my acquaintances, even after drinking too much alcohol could admit they were a mere nothing, just a Joe-Schmoe. Unless that someone could tell to his face one day, *Old man, you're a rubber.* And the man would get in a huff and go home to drink, but inside something would give him a cue that he actually is a rubber indeed.

I felt ashamed to live with those future multi-million deals. But I could not make myself out of bed in the morning otherwise. What was it all for, then? That would have been stupid.

Ilya never asked what I was doing, and how I was making my living. He knew all about it. He knew he would not be able to pull me out of my daily life, even if he wanted to. My life was dear to me, and I hated myself for it. Ilya never judged me for what I hated so badly within my own self.

I had never attempted to get closer to him. Ilya was no young man. He was hard on seventy. But his age wasn't telling on him, as if time had long ago stopped for him. Yet he had a habit of living alone. I was about forty, and also used to living alone. I didn't want to be a burden to him. Ilya made no calls. He called me when he couldn't come, to say, *I'm not coming, I'm busy.* And would never tell me, *I am not coming, I'm tired.* He was taking his rests with me.

My own life has not changed since the time I started going over to Ilya's.

I never asked Ilya of his doings. Why would I? His bank was in its final days. This was clear. So what could I ask? *Why go to the bank, dear? Shall we stay in bed a little longer?*

I never thought of where he was, and who he was meeting. I felt comfortable with him saying he missed me.

Ilya could throw me away, but just had no stomach. Or maybe he was just waiting for me to have enough of coming over: meanwhile I was waiting for him to have enough of me one fine day and kicking me away. So we just let it be as if floating down-stream. I had my evenings and nights with Ilya. I was cooking for him at the weekends, and greeted him at the house porch. We smoked sitting on that porch at nights, and in the mornings we would be drinking coffee on the terrace. There was nothing else I wanted.

All I had near and dear in my life was Ilya.

Ilya came in with his bodyguard. Boris was an elderly man. He looked like a businessman, but his motions were scarce, as if he was used to talking round corners. One could tell he was a retired serviceman and had served a long time in the West. He still kept the gloss of his well-fed lifestyle which had lost so many our servicemen in the years of immiseration. Boris greeted Marc as his oldie, making a wry face, dropped, *Why are you drinking this crap?* and they left to look at the intruder alarm equipment.

Ilya was standing in front of the cut-out glass in his guest room. It drew in the feeling of rawness from the riverside. It was totally dark in the street: heavy fog was raising from the ground, the blue in next door's neon advertising and the headlight beams of the passing cars, just like plumes of cigarette smoke. Due to the neon lights Ilya's face looked white like his shirt. I could see even the finest lines round his eyes, a couple of deep wrinkles cutting his sunken cheeks disappearing within the corners of his mouth, hiding the same lines of a smile. Still, his lips weren't smiling. He has calm and patronizing look in his grey eyes. So many people wishing to avoid that glance of his that would burn with ice-like metal in the frost. The bank staff fancied Ilya and feared him at the same time.

Coming back to his office Ilya shrugged with the cold, and asked me to make coffee, switching on his computer.

"You got scared, baby?" he asked. "I didn't want Marc to take you on with him."

"Yeah, I thought I'd wet my pants. He was just like a wild beast. He smelled my perfume."

"Well, he didn't tell you you've got your period coming tomorrow?" Ilya almost smiled.

"Oh fuck you, Ilya... " I couldn't get used to him having that keen antennae.

"So what the fuck did he come for?" Ilya asked this question as if he'd asked himself a hundred times before.

On his screen there came a message of a funds transfer to his bank.

"What the hell?" Ilya jumped to his feet, swore his head off and started calling his deputy chairman.

The bank accounts were getting filled back with the bad debt of the defense sector and the Third World countries that Ilya had sold not to spoil the bank balance, allegedly sold, as one could never sell the debt of Cuba, Morocco, Zimbabwe or the Congo. It all looked as if the debt had been purchased from his bank. In reality, it had all been purchased by Ilya's offshore company. He had dumped all of it over there just like to his waste-bin.

The return of these debts into his bank meant total disaster: the recall of his banking license.

CHAPTER THREE

THE DEBT

Ilya had acquired that debt with the bank. Some time ago, the bank used to be owned by a public company, and Ilya had taken over the chairman's office nominally. But after the collapse of the Soviet Empire, the company had withdrawn from the government tutorage, and the bank remained in his hands together with its bad debt and lawsuits from the foreign banks, that he saw no end of.

His deputy, a balding old man, as sleepy and wired as an alcoholic, entered the doors after fifteen minutes, yawning and wiping his sweaty hind-head with a handkerchief.

"Mother-fucker! What do we do?" asked the deputy, looking at the lines of the debt at the screen.

"Make a mirror offshore. Fast. Use the same name, easy jurisdiction. Damp all this debt over there. Then alter the bank details in all the contracts. Make it fast," Ilya ordered. "And... find out what is there with the company manager. He must be dead by now. Let someone contact the local police and his family. Get me through in case his wife or daughter picks up... "

"He's dead. There is no information yet," the deputy said dropping into Ilya's office two minutes later.

"Fuck'em all," Ilya told me irritantly, pouring Marc and me a cognac. "I never thought someone could break my bank in such a wonderful way..."

"Will the bank survive? The license won't get revoked?" Marc inquired.

"Oh yes, in the case that we can hide these debts. But the head of my damp company is dead now. This can't be for no reason, this is a multimode game. It has only just started."

"Why would someone break your bank?"

"Well, the easy option is kick the bank from its share in one of the five corporations. It happens when they discover rough diamonds or oil. Or when a big deal starts taking shape. Nobody's willing to share. So they get rid of the odd mouth," Ilya said.

"So how do you know?" Marc asked.

Ilya looked round his office, and his glance stuck to the broken window.

"You think, after all of this it makes sense my talking to anyone? Damn it. No way... You've got to go, Marc, get it straightened up with all of those companies."

"What am I looking for?"

"A major deal. A company getting rid of its founding parties. Three corporations rank in chain of clearing the bad government debt. Diamonds, oil and airlines. Two of those in Guinea. Start from those ones. Get a handle on those," Ilya handed him a list of five companies where the bank had a share.

"Why the bank has got so much of this African crap hanging on?"

"I wanted to somehow discharge the bad debts. I signed a contract with the head of all of these companies. Take Anna along with you. Let her talk first. I'll draw up a Power Of Attorney."

"Anna?" Mark asked again in surprise. "Ilya, do you want me to change her diapers or...?"

"Marc, I'm not sending over anyone from the bank as I'm sure there is nothing to talk about. This is not about talks. This is my personal warning. Anna will speak on my own behalf. Woman are easy to talk to, in case something..."

"She is not a woman, she's an errand boy," Marc put a value on me. "No one would ever talk to her."

"She's a middleman. She's used to handling daily talks with all kinds of shithead that keep fucking each other for half a percentage point."

"Is she living over in the dump?" Marc ascertained.

"Right. In the dump."

One day Ilya asked me,

"There is a schizophrenic going round the banks with a high-yield program. He's got on a pink tie, about sixty. Ever met him?"

"Yeah, I did. I flipped him right away."

"If I only could do the same. Had to listen to him for a good half hour. Then some other folks said they worked for the Secret Service and asked for a billion dollars in cash. That is half of the customer floor in the bank-packed wads. They came by Metro, fuck... "

And we laughed.

I was smoking at the broken window, watching the cigarette smoke mix with the chilly morning fog, almost paying no attention to their conversation. Ilya was scared for me, and to send me away.

"And how do they know she's your man?" insisted Marc.

"Well, we've been talking to you for about fifteen minutes now. Consider it business talks. Anna has been there with us. Would you understand she is my person?" Ilya asked.

"Yes," Marc gave way unwillingly. "A woman won't hold her tongue when someone is speaking about her."

"So what do you say, baby?" dropped Ilya.

He wasn't asking. It was damn clear from his tone he'd decided to say goodbye to me.

"Go fuck yourself, Ilya," I snapped discontentedly.

"I'm taking her," Marc agreed.

"Marc, in case she doesn't know something, she'll call me and ask what she should do. In the case she can't get through then take prompt action as needed. It does not really matter what she says there. The main thing is, – we get to see the company board tear ass... If we can do without much talking, that's even better."

Ilya hugged Marc and patted his shoulder. Then the door closed after Marc. His kiss felt bitter with cognac and cigarettes.

"Would you like to live with Ilya?" Mark asked taking the wheel.

"Yeah but... One day my friend, for whom I cook porridge for every morning all week long, could say, *I've got the money; let's go break the bank...* "

"Argh... so, raiding?"

"Yeah. And I don't know how long it could take and what would be the outcome of it. Ilya may not be able to wait for me until the end of the show. Or else I might end up in jail."

"You? In jail? Light me a cigarette," he asked somewhat puzzled.

"Oh yes, because the money would flow through my personal accounts."

"You are money laundering... " Marc nodded, drawing in on his cigarette.

"No, it's just for the bank."

"Is Ilya aware of it?"

"Nope."

"And how old is your friend there?"

Marc was driving fast, and I felt under my skin his piercing side-glance stuck to my face through the cigarette smoke. He would stare this way to know what he'd actually missed out.

"Sixty five. He's an expert in finance, as good as Ilya. Peter used to be Ilya's deputy. I'm involved with some friends of his. Making my money in modest transactions. Hardly making my living."

"And why?"

"We got to know each other when Peter was contemplating raiding Ilya's bank. Ilya had kicked him out. Today, no bank would have him on board."

"So what kind of relationship is that?"

"Much the best," I noticed Marc examine me again, hiding his gaze with the cigarette smoke, double-checking. "Ilya is taking a holiday with me, while Peter gives me a job. But that is not the point either. I'm a middleman, a mere nothing. And it's hard for a middle person to hold down a deal. With no backup with Peter, I would have died of hunger."

"Ilya doesn't give you cash?"

"Oh yeah, cash for fuel and cigarettes. Shall I light another one for you?"

I just wanted to say I was living with Peter the way I wanted, but then thought Marc would probably not understand.

This was a dump: all those old men on the street, most of them ex-quarterdeck. And all of them equally had nothing. However, they were of different breed. Some of them treated me in a friendly manner, others looked at me like thing they would wish to buy, but I was too expensive for them. And I didn't like the latter kind. They viewed everything this way. These were crushed and cautious down-to-earth people. They knew their limits at all times, and would judge just about anything within their limits. I couldn't understand this race, couldn't understand how they kept going to the office, getting their three-hundred-buck wages, and would be this way till the end of their life, not really daring to bank upon anything at all. They certainly seemed more solid in the public eye and probably more confident. But what could they be confident of? Of their coming pay-day? Of their familiar surroundings? The deuce only knows.

All of them have been long since living paycheck to paycheck, and living decently while these friends of mine were still crazy about ghostly millions.

It seemed just recently I didn't even wish to talk to them, pushing them away as if they were contagious.

However, one day I saw a steel case containing two ampoules of Selenium 74Se open before my eyes, and I've got the fever very much like delirium. I took an ampoule with my fingers that seemed not my own, and in a strange flat voice only asked,

"And where's the certificate?"

"Here it is."

I took the certificate copy into my hands, looked into the floated fax lines, and then said goodbye and left. I closed the door. And I felt the door of the madhouse ward close after me, so that I continue my living right there. That was what happened, actually. And giving up everything, I rushed like crazy to sell the selenium. Then I was also matched with oil, rough diamonds, Gazprom notes. I got used to it, grew on it, and acquired a taste for it. This life good for madmen only somehow settled down and resumed its natural course.

Peter and I rented a two-room apartment in the suburbs of Moscow, and it served us a broker's office.

Sometimes, when falling asleep, I kept turning in my mind all our day activities, rising from my bed, opening the door a crack to Peter's room inquired,

"Are you sleeping there? Have you sold the oil?"

"Oh shit, it just went out of my mind," he responded and got up to make another call.

So every day I was getting off to his talking on the phone. In the morning I woke up with a telephone call and Peter's voice,

"This one is for you. So what have you failed to sell yesterday?"

A year ago Peter was thinking he could manage to take a loan in a Western bank, big enough to undertake a takeover of some bank on the verge of its license revocation. He could actually make arrangements with a foreign investor, – it had actually happened before, – but he was in debt to the armpit and didn't want to take risks. Time passed by, but he still had no credit line open, and this wouldn't hurt us in any way. I loved this life. With Peter being there it hadn't really changed much: my contacts only grew more high-profile. For us together the whole thing was lively. I was thinking maybe Ilya felt more comfortable with Peter looking after me, even if we never discussed these things.

I liked the dump I lived in, actually. I liked my every fucking day.

Or maybe, the mischief of it was that I couldn't imagine what my days would be like with Ilya.

"If Ilya offered to me to live happily ever after, not just over the weekend at the summerhouse... Hmm... He is unlikely to say so... but then I don't mind if I do."

I might say one day, *I cannot come over to you Ilya, and I've got a job to do.*

I think he'll reply, *Leave me the key then, I won't be waiting for you.*

Anyway, whatever I have with Ilya, it seemed we had no chance to stay together.

"So the matter is not about Ilya, it's probably you."

"I don't know, Marc. If I only knew why we are together with Ilya... I know this summerhouse has never had women, before me... I don't know what to think," I've been thinking it over a thousand times and still got no answer.

"Right, there have never been any women. Same for his apartment. He used to rent a flat for women... used to do so before," Marc cautiously said through his teeth.

"For women... I know there have been many," I smiled. "I'm not jealous, Marc. If Ilya has somebody else, he'll tell me. Or I'll feel it."

"Then this is affection indeed."

"Ilya said this is not love, but rather an instinct. Just like what wild animals have sensing each other from a long distance."

"Has Ilya been courting you?" Marc was hardly looking at me, but under his close inspection I was feeling like a bug pinned to a board.

I couldn't understand why he was questioning me. Looking at his face, bloated and white with the highway lights, and the shadows running across it like in shallow waters, I caught myself thinking it was quite easy speaking to him about things I was reluctant to tell to myself. I felt comfortable with him. I started smoking dissolved into laughter:

"No. I'm courting him. Marc I don't like questions. Shall we just punch each other in the face?"

"There's plenty of time yet... And still... "

"I'm afraid Ilya does not really need me. What for? To cook him supper?"

"And what if you don't cook supper?" Marc snorted and broke into a grin.

"I think he'll take his shotgun off the wall and smash my head off," I smiled. "But I want him."

"You'll get fuck all... So you are actually chasing him?"

What could I say? Ilya loved Hungarian meat. He loved sex, as soon as he opened his summer place door Friday night, coming from his bank. He wanted to fuck his mind away from his job. He loved smoking a cigar with a cup of coffee in the morning on the terrace. He also liked my hungry eyes there. We loved to walk in the woods or travel some place. He loved that vacation home. In summer we went to Switzerland, and spent a whole month in the countryside.

"Yeah. Marc, is Ilya somewhat scared for me?"

"Oh, really? I wouldn't count on that," he responded, and I felt better right along.

"I've seen that gunman. And you've seen him too. He's come to the bank so he can actually come anywhere."

"Yes, we got to find him. I think he's not getting in on the act. He's no peg boy contracted to break into the bank. He may be involved with some company. So we are looking for the company."

The silence seemed embarrassing. Marc smiled:

"Feel free to entertain me with babble. I'm at the wheel. It's barely three o'clock in the morning. Or you'd rather I dose off? Light me a cigarette there."

"Marc... I noticed Boris kind of envies you... " I lit him a cigarette.

"I'm a slacker. I don't go to the same shop for my vodka. I don't air the dog at the same time of night in front of my house. And this will probably save my life. And Ilya is as safe, as he's got no rules."

"Oh, that is true," I agreed.

"By the way, I love vodka."

"Me too."

"Care for a drink?"

"Yeah. We've got the flight anyway."

And then we took a flight to Haifa.

CHAPTER FOUR

GUINEA

The company Levin & Berg, with its humble offices in the far suburbs of Haifa, was trading in rough diamonds, and had just got a license for oil lease on the deep shelf of Guinea.

Marc intended to observe the company offices from the abandoned floor of the industrial building opposite. After talking to the company dean Michael Levin I was supposed to take a taxi and go to the airport straight away. However walking into the square and looking at the company building, Marc decided there was no point to take so much risk. Apparently the company was spending a potful of money on security and I had to go unattended. Marc said if he stayed somewhere in the area he'd get spotted in a few minutes.

We didn't stay in the hotel and didn't rent a car; we were just strolling around the deserted city. Because of the time difference we both felt disinclined for sleep.

In the morning the sand and dust rose just like dense fog, one couldn't see the sun, the sky looked void. Everything around us was lit with the steady blurred, dazzling, light. The incoming traffic under the city bridge offended the eye with its vivid glare.

Marc looking over my jeans and T-shirt and asked,

"So you go that way?"

"I could wear a jacket, but I'd rather Levin not think of me as a manager. You know they put down the managers."

I entered the café before the company building across the road at opening time, ordered a coffee, smoked a cigar, and then inquired if the waiter knew Levin. It turned out Levin had his lunch here daily, and asked the waiter to invite Levin to my table once he came in. The company executive car came very soon. I waved my hand to Levin as soon as the waiter pointed at me.

Levin, lean and grey-haired, faded like the grass in the sun and nine-lived like a pike: you could roast him yet every single piece would still twitch. He took his seat opposite me. It crossed my mind only retired colonels could die-hard like this.

"Nice to meet you. You must be the wife of Ilya Ivanovich?" This was no question, actually.

"Nice to meet you too, Mr. Levin. Is Ilya Ivanovich married?" I smiled.

"No but... " he curled his lips in a sympathetic grin, "A girlfriend would be young, taller, sexier..."

"I'm just a middleman."

"No. Not so many women smoke a Havana with a cup of coffee. That's unlike a manager. If any of my managers smoked this kind of cigar, I would think he is robbing me blind. You are smoking habitually. Then you've been a long time with Ilya... Well, let us not lose time. I heard something happen to the bank. Shall we go up to my office?"

"No, thank you. I'm here for a few words only. The bank hasn't suffered. Things will remain as they were. Do I have to know if you plan company board changes?"

"I'd be glad to reply that this is not the business where things change. However the bank, where I took a loan, just like other oil companies on the same block, actually wants to drive me to bankruptcy. I haven't started my drilling yet. I even don't know if there is any oil in there. And those who've started, they got little or none."

"That means... "

"That means you just came on time. The bank has filed a suit against us. In this case the bank is to be handled by Ilya Ivanovich."

"Why haven't you told him before?"

"Because normally one could reassign the debt and reach an arrangement of some kind. But the bank won't budge. So call your legal advisor... In the event anything happened to Ilya Ivanovich, I would go bankrupt."

"Why haven't you started drilling?"

"Someone broke into my office and forced the safe. We had to spend all the money to install the security."

He invited me to be his guest any time and suggested to take me to the airport.

"No-no, thanks. Nice to meet you, Mr. Levin."

Marc and me, we took different flights.

"We won't find out much here," Marc said, when we met in the transit area. "He either made enquiries about Ilya, or can see you through to naked. What do you think of that asshole?"

"Nobody knows I'm actually involved with Ilya. One could only find out by tracking Ilya... Suppose he did the tracking?... I believe it is in his interest to pretend he has no clue to who I am, and talk to me some more to learn what I know. Levin is a rude son-of-a-bitch enjoying himself. And I liked it. Did you call Ilya?"

"Yep, he said he'd handle this. And we are heading to Guinea meanwhile."

"Why?"

"There are aircraft. They could have been caught on fair-trade. Let's see."

We went into the airfield, where the dust smell overtook all the gasoline odors. The dust was so thick in the air one could almost swallow it.

Marc washed his mouth with gin, taking a swig from his bottle and gave it to me,

"Take a gulp so as not to catch malaria. And start smoking – there's hardly a breath in the air. This is the blackest asshole I've ever had to get out from. I like it. And you'll like it. Keep drinking your gin more often."

I asked him why, and regretted my asking. Marc said that everything one is used to: culture, reputation, good conscience, and other pompous triviality that only men with full stomachs could afford, would get lost right away over there; it would shell off just like old paint off the fence. There are rotting clothes sticking to skin wounds that never heal, black flies eating you alive, the never-ending diarrhea, and the heat making your brain boil and your memory burn out, and the lust for hallucinations. Once you start rotting alive as a corpse decays in the sun, you turn into what you actually are: a wild beast.

Oleg the airline owner came out of the air-shed greeted us, and said all of his cargo flights had been booked out for the month to come.

"We are from Ilya Ivanovich, Oleg. Just a drive-by visit. No accreditation. That is, in case your founding members are the same... How are you doing there?"

"Fucking great... Only, it seems as though I got my business no more, it's taken-over debt by the casino. I've gambled it away," Oleg said.

"Well, I called the lawyer. Tomorrow we plead before a court."

"What's your lawyer saying?"

"I'll lose it. Said, they'd planted on their own advisor when I was signing the debt acknowledgement."

"Okay, we'll wait until your lawyer comes."

We took a seat at the table in the air-shed.

Oleg had been the company director for a long time. He had strong links with the defense companies, he owned a fleet of aircrafts, and could still make a bigger offer, but it was impossible to wheedle money out of the local government. It seemed they didn't realize the Soviet Union was not there anymore.

"They wouldn't fund nor guarantee anything. They want it the same Soviet era way. They've actually got no budget for the air program. My navigation office in Moscow allowed for all possibilities. And these niggers... I'm sick and tired of... Losing paperwork, seals, phone numbers, their own wives.... Every single day that nigger walks with a beaten face, his car stolen, his passport lost, his wife left, " Oleg smiled. "And all of it within one week! White man can hardly take it in. And it's fine with them. In the case a Russian businessman got into that kind of trouble, people would think there's something wrong with him. There's not a single delivery order to be paid in money, just order forms. I've got everything ready, the aircraft, the pilots and the routes. But a flight has to be paid at least with an insurance deposit, or by letter of credit mode. And these guys have got no an insurance deposit either.

They'd never get customers that way. It's absurd. You won't believe it. I had to give up the passenger flights. Someone is working with them. I can't. Imagine those niggers cross the border control and Customs that side without any problem and here they come out of the plane without a passport! Claiming it got lost on the flight! Then they scatter from the transit zone. And you got to watch them as a bunch of pricks, so they don't spread out. I got a friend that carries Arabs. He also gets the Afghans. They actually play the Arabs. And every flight the Anti-Terrorist Squad comes to close off the passenger area, shake them all down, and that happens to every flight. Whatever you do, take their passport away to make their mugs look like those passport photos. One comes with a passport and leaves with another. They are black, all the same. You can't really sort them out, can you?"

While he was speaking, I thought of myself. The trench coat I was wearing, I'd been wearing for five years, my boots were totally worn out ... And my contacts were in trouble just like those 'niggers':

their wives had left, their faces were beaten, and their car stolen...

"There is no law. Conning The Whites is a holy cause. They've got friends. They've got the clan. You may save his life. Do for him whatever... But their ruling tribe is cannibalistic. And I am big and white. And whatever paperwork you've got there signed, you get eaten. Well yes, you save his life and make friends forever, and then his holiday comes around, and his family member says you got to be their barbeque there," Oleg smiled.

"Oh yeah, you somewhat fumble and oops, you've got him hanging over your head, his balls hanging to your eyes, those fucking black balls!" Marc laughed.

"They really don't know to respect people. They only know fear. If you fumble a bit, they kill you. The Ukes safeguard us, me and a friend of mine, a local mine owner. He's lucky not to see those niggers at all. They won't let the niggers within shot of him. They understand they are in a cannibal country, and have got no backing space. And so they hold them off at gunpoint.

The Ukrainians are another tribe, but they know to handle a weapon... and could easily kill anyone there. They take horilka against the yellow jack."

Listening to Oleg, me and Marc we exchanged looks and made another gulp of gin.

"There should be adequate whites to make things work here."

"So the company situation is just the same?" I asked.

"Yes. I would add up some more aircraft. But I find it difficult to make an arrangement with the Embassy in Moscow, getting the paperwork required and at bank account number. And I can't find a trustee for the bank good enough for VTB to open an account. They need aircraft, sporting planes as well as freight carriers. The niche is there, the market is available. I've got the aircraft leasing for shipment arranged. But who pays? That may be whoever but not the blacks. So I'm saying there should be some whites to make it all work out. The clans keep changing, and they scrape it off, all those people who used to work in the niches. People come to disappear. In case someone on top is replaced, they get to scrape off everyone under his management."

"Oleg, so what do you carry?" Marc asked.

"Wire cable, mining equipment... Can't really load nuts or fish, which could leak. The customers are French and Italian."

"So why won't they finance it? Are these regular customers?"

"I'm in debt," Oleg took a paper out of his locker filled with figures and dates.

Marc, hardly looking at it inquired:

"How far is the casino?"

The lawyer, a cheeky old man with two bodyguards came by at night. After talking to him, we decided the bank could go into the company administration for the time of the proceedings. The proceedings wouldn't take long there. It could be done in one day; in the case we hurried up we could funnel all the company assets and leave the casino with a dummy. Tell it all to the casino owner, and he most probably agrees for the bank to repay the debt.

In local terms the debt amount seemed huge: one hundred thousand dollars.

However Ilya used to carry something with Oleg's company, and could still carry something and that were no bananas.

Anyways, the bank went into the company administration.

At the post-office, exchanging email agreements with the bank I told Marc with regret,

"We have found out nothing yet and already got into debt. I don't think the matter is this company. We are losing time handling all this."

CHAPTER FIVE

TWILIGHT

We had to stay there for another day to get the paperwork done.

The twilight was as brief as a psychopath's thought. The setting sun instantly burnt everything around us. The dark was blinding. The recent light was still in our eyes. As soon as the eye started detecting the lustrous aluminum roof of the air-shed, the darkness came live. The noises changed into the anxiety and breathing of the close neighborhood, and somewhere nearby the sound of a repressed sigh; it felt just like at madhouse corridor by night. In the wind-blown metal air-shed, where we were spending the night, every sound thumped the walls, shaking them with an echo.

Marc was drinking gin without getting drunk. What a bummer. The hotspot of the lighter was burning in his eyes. He lit a cigar and let me take a pull. Marc warned me not to eat anything. I had no wish to eat. In the deadly heat my sweat kept salting through the T-shirt seams, which then dried and cut into sore skin. Every gulp of gin went down my throat in blistering cold to the stomach, and then straight to the bladder.

"I'm actually scared to wee over here; something could bite my ass... "

"Don't use the torch, or the neighborhood crowd will rush out to have a look at it. They love the light. Shall I stand by with a gun with you while you wee?" he laughed out loud, protruding his wet lip.

"I was thinking of a sniper rifle... Marc, where are you from?" I asked, almost falling asleep.

"Boston. I served in the Marine Corps, long time back, some thirty years ago. Since then I have been living in Moscow."

"Really? Missing those times?"

Had he never mentioned it, I would never have guessed he was an American.

"Nope. If I stayed there, I would never know anything about myself... I've got no regrets. If I had to go over it again, I would do it. You have no idea... When we hunted out five bottles of gin, a Kalashnikov and a gas canister... Never been happier in my whole life," his bared white teeth flashed in a sharp grin.

"Where was that?"

"Over there, behind those mountains," Marc waved his hand in the bay direction.

"Marc, thirty years back one could not get to Moscow from Boston. Were you a spy or something?"

"Yes, that was long time ago. There used to be a fishing base over here, no diplomatic mission. There started some kind of uproar, or a take-over, in a nutshell, one darky took off with all the treasury funds. Our carrier anchored in the bay; we were four with the senior officer. We had to find that guy, off the record. So we covered some distance; it was hard to make more than ten-fifteen kilometers a day across these mountains. We found the darky in his Land Rover, or what actually there remained of him. The bags filled with dollars remained intact. Out of us four riflemen, I was the only one that survived. When I came to my senses I could only see the other boys' bodies torn apart to the bones. There was no signal. I took the way back. The recovery team of ten riflemen immediately took our track. They found me a kilometer from those others. I kept throwing up and couldn't stop, they started throwing up as soon as they saw them too. We came back and none of us on board could eat a morsel. I couldn't even climb on board, throwing up. The physician on board left me onshore with a nurse. I entered the shed, took a look at the cooling fans on the ceiling and got to throwing up again."

"That was cannibals?"

"Yes, everyone knew they harbored in the area. Some nights they came down to the village. People got used to them just like the wild animals in the neighborhood. They were just the same; invisible, predaceous inhumans.

None of the people on the base had ever seen them, or could remember anything like that case. The commanding officer smoked a cigarette with me but I couldn't speak to him. And then they requested an analyst from Headquarters; he came with the air carrier along with the mail. His name was Allen Norman. He spent four hours talking to me, asking why those cannibals hadn't hurt me, kept asking and asking. He had to do the questioning as he had to report it to a Special Agent. There was no way to explain things to him. Whatever I said, whatever the analyst told him, he still decided I had killed my buddies there. I was lucky the doctor got me all right and could somehow have it out with the Agent. At least I was left in peace onshore for the night."

"Why didn't the cannibals touch you, Marc?"

"They must have felt I was one of them. The same gut feeling animals have," Marc was wary in the choice of words. "I told the same to the analyst, and that was probably wrong. But that time I couldn't think straight."

"Marc, you mean they felt you being just like them, a cannibal?" I asked bluntly, coming out of soak.

"Yes. That's the underlying sense."

"So what happened next?" I asked, rising my glass of gin to take a gulp.

"Then came Ilya, he came for me."

"Ilya? Ilya ever been here? With you?" I thought I must have misheard.

"Yes. We arranged it that Ilya would meet me whenever I could pry away from that team of mine... They were all dead, but I still couldn't leave them, and came back. I couldn't go back to those woods either. Ilya came to take me and we left together. I wouldn't have sustained it without him. So he had been walking through these fucking woods alone... And we found five bottles of gin together with him."

"That all sounds horrible, Marc... So you met Ilya... "

"Ilya was a sleeper agent... He had to take me to the Soviet Union. That was a long time back... "

"So you live next door to Ilya's vacation home because... "

"...Ilya has passed word for me. And then he bought that summerhouse for me."

"So you... ergh... I'd better not sleep there?" I made a silly joke thickly.

"You sleep. I won't eat you. Shall we drink some more?" suggested Marc.

"Okay. *For those in the shade*, if you don't mind?"

A friend of mine, an ex-intelligence officer, used to get angry with me if I ever offered this toast to him too lightly.

"You're an idiot... "

He laughed. And his laughter resounded there with a barking cough from outside the wall in a dull echo.

CHAPTER SIX

THE DEAL

The next day in the hotel nearby the airport I felt totally done in the morning after. My body was aching in its goofy dead-weight, and sweat under my skin like melting snow was, still not melting. The stifling steam heat hadn't eased off all night, giving no chance to sleep. Towards morning I had a nightmare.

I saw Marc in the door way, sober, with his hair wet after at shower, in a white T-shirt stuck to his bloated belly, his loutish smile on, and yesterday seemed to have been total bullshit.

"You want some? No headache the morning after?" he asked, taking a gulp of gin straight from the bottle.

"Yeah, somewhat. Headache is there."

"That's okay. I was afraid you'd catch malaria. I'll get down to the café, bring something for lunch."

Marc left. I opened the laptop and typed: Doctor Allen Norman.

On his website there was his biography and a few chapters from his book *The Jackal: The Psychology of Terror.*

That was a crude and clear psychological theory. One could make a wolf from a dog, but couldn't ever make a dog of a wolf. A wolf is born to be a wolf and will die a wolf. In the case all wolves get shot, and there is only one female wolf left, she'd find herself a dog, and after four generations those wolf cubs will have no trace of the dog species, and become pure-blooded wolves. The predators' gene pool is actually stronger.

Sometime in the past, humans used to fall into two groups of predatory humans and common humans. They still remain that way. Among people there are still some predatory humans, and in this group there features more cruelty, ambition, and a need to dominate. That is in a few words the essence of that theory.

In primeval times a human could only kill another human, as wild animals would rapidly scatter away from him. So just like our predecessors, we keep eating dead things, buying them from the supermarket. No wolf eats a dead wolf; no band will march against another band. Man is different from animals, because the olden days he used to kill his like. As per this theory the predatory race used to breed another kind of human in cattle folds, just like pigs, to provide foodstuff.

The brain of a common human is made to obey the command suppressing its instinct of self-preservation, and eventually they get killed. The word is believed to inhibit the brain response. The power of suggestion is in the compulsory force of the word. And the words are perceived as commands. We either obey or protest, human conversation is all about exchange of mutual protest. The first ever speech was no information exchange, but pure commands. The predatory human is, quite the opposite, seeming not to hear any words and assigning no meaning to words. Their frontal cortex area remains rudimentary. So they trust their instincts only, and live as wild beasts.

Supposedly, the word could slow down the instincts and thus hinder the first human survival. However, Natural Selection makes no allowance for any features that may be harmful. So this feature turned out rather effective... for the strong to subdue the weaker ones. The modern human has been accidentally evolved from his predatory counterparts. In escaping their predatory counterparts the first humans settled all over the world. They were scattered not by cold, but fear. And those who escaped earlier and settled a greater distance from the predators became restrained in their mental development, like the tribes of the Far North or Native Americans, while those bound to live by the predators actually progressed. The fear of their predatory counterparts has become the force for their mental growth. Settling further away, the first humans started speaking their own language to define their fellow-countrymen, and not to understand the words of a stranger that could be a predator. They protected themselves with this foreign-language incomprehension from their predatory counterparts.

All people are different, but this is not about their race. One could easily go past a predator taking no notice.

I should say these things were common knowledge made aware quite thoroughly by Doctor Norman.

"The Jackal lives by his code, his code having nothing to do with the code of the rest of the world," I was reading the chapter under my breath, "but when you know the code no harm can come to you."

It was amazing. So the story Marc told me was no fantasy of his heat-boiled brain.

"So you think the matter is not the company?" Marc asked when we sat down to lunch.

"Marc, all those companies are so small. Even that business of Levin. They are not fit for the big money. If someone poured cash to find out Ilya had an offshore company that no bank people know of... that requires major turnover.

It seems to be the bank that offered credit to Levin and now wants to get rid of him."

"You think Levin is in trouble?"

"Yes."

Marc's cell beeped. That was Ilya,

"Marc, the company may have nothing to do with it, there is a bank... "

One bank had a share of all the oil companies in one block on the deep shelf of Guinea. The point was, in contrast to the Angolan shelf here, in Guinea there were more lots without oil. Apparently, the oil companies that had started drilling in block had either found nothing or very little volume. It's not hard to understand it was Levin had oil without being aware of it. The bank-creditor to all those oil companies realized his debtors would never pay him back. In case they drove Levin's company to bankruptcy and got his license withdrawn, they could pump as much oil as they wanted to cover the losses.

"So what do we do?" Marc inquired from Ilya.

"Nothing. I know who is playing against me and why. I'll take some time to think what to do.

Get some rest," said Ilya.

Ilya, dumping all of his bad debts into one sewer company still made some effort to clear all the same.

The government debt was issued in bills. These bills were bought out by a broker company that was reselling the same to the lessee of the oil-bearing shelf lot. The latter was the small company of Levin. Levin had partially paid his license in those bills to the public corporation in charge of such license issue. As for the bills, he was supposed to make a deferred payment upon the sale of his oil.

Ilya had in his bank along with these debts quite a few similar and even more complicated schemes with rough diamonds. Basically, one had plenty of choice.

"You wanna blast my brain?" asked Marc.

"Marc, it's all clear enough. Levin took on a loan from the bank, backed by his exploration license. In the case he does not pay it back, he goes bankrupt. And his license gets withdrawn by the bank. However, there is a fine point. In case the company goes bankrupt, the payment liability lies with a miserable third-rate bank in Moscow that has not a single dollar in its account, but tons of junk bonds in which he would actually settle on the company's behalf. So the bank-creditor sends over a nutcase with a Zippo lighter to break that Moscow bank together with its junk bonds. Then makes the oil company bankrupt, and starts drilling. So what's the bank name?"

I opened my laptop and we gazed into the screen. I could stay a week longer there just examining the Standard Investment Bank website, and its homepage photo showing the flow of people past the glass doors into the streets of Antwerp.

"Have you got any contact to arrange us a personal meeting with the banker? No? And so I thought," Marc sniffed.

"Marc, and in olden times the KGB servicemen used to have their showers, shaves, and dentistry done before their visit to the bank, when needed... "

"Yep, and were also issued a briefcase with a million dollars in cash ... And now we've got none."

"Marc, I know Ilya would not talk to anyone, not even in the court room. And he's got no money for the proceedings. I can only guess how mad Ilya is."

"Oh yes, and I've had all those lawyers for breakfast," Marc smacked his lips.

We kept silent for a while, had the rest of the gin. It seemed an eternity had passed. I felt feeble and feckless. Marc took out another bottle of gin.

"Marc, what if we put on ski masks, take the shotguns..."

"...And enter a voided bank. It granted credit to a number of oil businesses and got nothing, so it's no better than ours... "

"Gosh, Ilya is left with nothing... Why would Ilya hold onto his Moscow bank?"

"Or maybe he loves his summerhouse?" Marc responded and I regretted my asking.

"Yeah, really, I didn't think of that... "

"But we both know where to look for that Zippo gunman. In the Standard Investment Bank."

"Marc, the ugly thing is, in case something goes not the way the bank wants that man could come again. Any place. That is, just behind Ilya's back. Marc, you'd better go stay with Ilya. He does need bodyguards... I don't know. You'll go right now, please. What if we don't find the Zippo guy?"

"No idea, it never happened before," Marc remarked as if taking pity on me. "Ilya's got a bodyguard. You remember? Ilya is fine. And you are not. You hardly get killed, but they may take you hostage to press on Ilya. So you stay glued to my side, not for a wee. You got me?"

"Yeah. Shall you keep me handcuffed to you?"

"You make a step away – I kill you. Whatever Ilya makes out, in case we find no Zippo guy to anchor him to the bank, Ilya won't have the lever."

Marc picked up the phone; it was Ilya,

"Marc I'm running into two billion debts. We'll have to hire the best lawyers and pay them up the wazoo, or maybe purchase the bank... I'm on my flight to Haifa."

"I think Ilya needs nothing, he's got his own way to get things done," Marc said. "We fly to Haifa."

We met Ilya in Haifa, in Levin's office, in the company, which actually was almost owned by Ilya.

Ilya took a round of the building. The offices appeared very much like an emergency shelter. All the vault door locks had several security features. Levin has smelled it was time to defend himself.

"Nice place for a meeting with the Standard Investment Board," Ilya noted, having a look at the conference hall, running his hand over the steel blinds on the windows, and peering at the mirror-like bare sky.

We climbed up to have a smoke on the roof.

"This is risky," Marc told him. "We haven't yet found that Zippo cracker."

"They'll tell us where to search," Ilya smiled.

CHAPTER SEVEN

THE DOMINO

From Haifa Ilya went to Geneva, to visit MLHK bank, which was the major creditor of the Standard Investment. He actually required no audit for these talks. It was obvious the audit would disclose that the Standard Investment was in trouble due to low-quality debtors such as those oil companies. The auditor would have warned the bank clients of the risks.

The Standard Investment Bank investing into the oil businesses was not able to not repay what was due to its major creditor MLHK. The debt amount was two billion.

Ilya was ready to take upon himself the responsibility for this debt and pay it off from his company oil sales and from the payments some other oil companies would make in the future. The credit volume for the oil companies on the Guinea shelf was almost two billion. In brief, Ilya assumed the default risk. This was a good offer to MLHK.

The Standard Investment had to assign to Ilya the receivables on the credit facility agreement with the borrowing oil companies.

Ilya was making money on the deferred payment.

By capturing the Standard Investment, its debtors and the creditor, Ilya was actually taking up everything the bank owned. He was ready to purchase a small bank right there in Antwerp. Still he was also ready to let it lie in the Standard Investment subject to him overtaking sixty percent of the bank shares.

Ilya didn't have to discuss things with the Standard Investment. The talks were handled by MLHK advisors. And it didn't take long.

But there was more to it.

From Geneva Ilya flew to Haifa. Through his attorney he offered the Standard Investment Board to hold a meeting in Haifa, in the Levin & Berg offices. They could not refuse.

Coming out of the car next to the Levin & Berg offices Ilya plunged into the heavy heat of the midday highway that respired in his face with hot asphalt and dust odors. His upper lip beaded with sweat, a hot wave pushed him in the back and glued his shirt to his body. He appeared weary and on edge.

"Do you play Russian-style chess?" the attorney of the Standard Investment asked Ilya, meeting him at Levin's company gate.

"This is a domino game. I'm taking your major creditor, and paying him. The rest of your bank's clients will leave following him, one by one."

When he got to the second floor, the whole Board of the Standard Investment was in the small conference room, two rows of impeccable young men, the management and the attorneys, all of them in expensive suits with a sharply white line of collar and a dull shoe luster, the glitter in their eyes, that would cautiously shine on the fringe and then go out again. Closer to the empty chair at the top of the table there was the bank's top management of old men, most of them Jewish, with receding hairlines, silver temples, crooked noses, and black bird-like eyes.

Ilya entered the room, with a sign requesting his attorney stay in the entry hall.

"By the end of this discussion you'll tell me who broke into my bank."

Ilya drew the steel blinds down the windows, and lifting a chair, took a swing and hit off the manual lock. The blinds shivered and grated against the window-sill, fixed dead. Ilya walked out and shut the door.

He asked the secretary to bring him some water, turned round, took the door handle and pushed, but it didn't open.

His face showed no surprise.

The attorney standing in the entry hall by the window, somewhat confused, took out a cigarette, twirled it in his fingers, and nervously dropped at Ilya,

"You could have warned me."

"Don't worry, this had happened before. If it

doesn't get rectified within half an hour we'll call a welder and cut out the lock. You may go smoke on the roof."

Early in the game it all seemed a folly. Last time we'd entered the conference room, with Ilya saying he'd get the Board locked in the room just like rats in a trap, I was thinking we'd never come out of the courts thereafter. The truth was Ilya had the money for the courts while his opponents had none.

So the doors closed behind Ilya and we sat in the next room to listen what they got to talking about.

Their cell phones were jammed and the landlines inside were cut off.

Two or three minutes went in perfect silence. It seemed the mike got switched off. They kept silent. And their silence seemed to be eternal, as if there was a dead body on the table. Then we could hear some shuffle of the shoes, squeak of the chair, a slight squeal of someone's cufflink against the table and the bang of elbows put on the table. It appeared one could listen to the silence. Their self-possession was amazing.

The rats locked in a can are said to devour the weakest one among them. This is not exactly true. The sick one gets eaten.

It didn't take them long to think things over. Many of the bank's top management owned the shares or some interest in other companies. And they ran the same directly or through their nominees. For their sake they were ready to act against the bank's interests. It was no hardship to detect the person who'd wheedled the money out of the bank for his own oil businesses. It was still not clear whether they found it hard to part with the man. Anyway, giving out just one person the rest of them would save face and their seat. That is, not to mention the bank was no more theirs.

We could hear a chair briskly move and the footfall of a single man. The blinds shivered and trembled under the hand blow.

"We are ready to talk," said the general manager, looking around the room in search of a camera.

Ilya called the security for them to get the door

open.

He chose not to talk to them. When his attorney entered the room, from the half-open door we could see one person stand with his face to the window, seizing the blinds and nestling his head against the same.

"Well," noticed Ilya once we went onto the roof to smoke a cigarette, "I was thinking I'd have to serve them all pizza first and then send them packing."

In a minute we had his attorney call, *Twenty per cent is yours. Come to sign the agreement.*

"I'm coming," Ilya said smiling, touching on Marc's shoulder to say goodbye. "You speak to that rat, and then leave for the airport."

"Ilya what if... " I didn't know how to word my being scared for him.

"This part is stipulated therein, in case they don't get to love me, my share shall be assigned to my Moscow bank along with the crap, debts and lawsuits."

"So where are you heading?" I asked.

"Antwerp. To have a look at my bank. See you

at home, baby," Ilya kissed me and went to the conference room.

I stared after him, his round shoulders and smooth gait, and felt acute hunger just like every time I saw him leave.

After Ilya left the room following the board members, Marc entered the room. He found nothing good talking to the rat.

There was a middleman between him and the Zippo guy. He paid cash to the middleman. He named the man in Ilya's bank who sold him the details of the offshore company, where Ilya had dumped all of his bank bad debts.

"Damn," Marc swore his head off, "Ilya has fixed it all for me. And I can't do anything. I feel like a complete banana."

CHAPTER EIGHT

AUTUMN

When Marc and I came back to Moscow it was autumn.

Breathing in the smells of the molten road tar and gas, I felt swollen up by the city again, eaten away and thrown out. I was leaving the place and thinking, I'd better not see it again. Moscow is a big city, you respond to a two dozen calls a day and then ask yourself toward the evening, *So who's that bitch who didn't call me today?* As if every dog there came to know me there. And I'd missed Moscow when I wasn't there, and this longing was for what would probably never happen again.

From afar Moscow seemed like a potato field, it expanded right in front of my eyes, and started swallowing in, breathing out with its rotten gut. Nothing had changed. The bank came out fine.

Ilya didn't call for a week long. Friday at noon I went to his summerhouse as usual. The autumn devastated his apple garden, through the nude branches one could see the neighbors' fence wet with the rain, the down and out vegetable patches, the woods beyond. The bullis vine leaves fell off the porch, and the terrace, dark with the leaves, grew somewhat lighter. The petty glass triangles were showing more of the dirty rain streaks.

It was clear Ilya hadn't been there for the two months me and Marc were traveling.

I didn't realize before how much it had all decayed over there. Maybe due to the yellow lamp-shades the room seemed to be evenly lit with the golden dust. All those things reflected just like that yellow light the patina of desolation and downfall, same as the bare faded fields along the roadway. Looking round I skittishly ran my hand over my face, I caught thinking I could not remember how it looked. How it looked there. Gazing into the mirror I saw myself in the dim yellow light as if from afar, totally different. I had the feeling of living in that house for many years.

Marc came in the morning and lit up the fireplace. The doors were wide open and the stale air of the house got mixed up with the smoke and the autumnal humidity.

I was making lunch, we drank gin waiting for Ilya.

The Zippo gunman never came back. Marc managed to track him down. He had his share in the bank. Had Ilya no access to the bank documents we would have never spotted him out.

I was asking why Ilya had been living alone all this time. Why wouldn't he have a family? Maybe, he didn't want any bonds to make his close ones suffer because of him. Or was he scared of the blackmail that he couldn't do anything about? Or had he experienced something of the kind? I knew this kind of fear well enough; my father used to have the same.

One day I asked Ilya about it. Ilya, at first brushing me aside, told me he wasn't scared for me, as it would be silly to fear for a cat enjoying its game on the highway. I was stubbornly waiting for his response.

"In case it happens you sit and waiting for me, I'll surely come. I kill you myself. You won't die alone, I promise. You wanna ask me some more questions?"

"No, Ilyusha, I'm sorry."

Since I didn't have to remember this conversation anymore and think about it, I found it easier to breath. Or maybe that was just the sharp autumn air with the bitter earth odor.

I didn't know what Ilya would say, but I was with him and I knew why I was with him there.

In the evening Ilya came. Coming out onto the porch to greet him, I saw him walking across the yard. From afar his face was looked tired, but as he approached it changed in front of my very eyes he became his usual self.

"I was missing... baby," Ilya stammered in a way I thought was his last time to call me baby. Giving Marc a hug, he said,

"Marc, this time I shouldn't have taken Anna along."

"I should tell you, you'd better live like you always lived, alone. You're getting old, Ilya... "

Fuck them all. Marc was right. If I hadn't been there it would have been easier for Ilya.

Relieved, I was thinking if I told Ilya now I got a job taking all my time preventing me from coming there at weekends, everything would be over. So that both of us could feel better.

Sunday night at dinner table I told him,

"Some job came up there for Peter. Someone wants a bank. So he's hiring us for the raid, and so... I won't be coming next weekend," I wasn't sure how to phrase it and feared for the answer.

"I'll help you out," Ilya said matter-of-factly, as if expecting something like that.

"I need no help," I snapped with surprise.

"Not you, you silly girl, since you don't really know what you are running into. Let Peter give me a call. He'll for sure need some help. And you, please come over Friday, make me dinner. Or I kill you."

Interview with Anna Schlegel, Author of THE DEAD BANK DIARY

I: Why the series' title is THE DEAD BANK DIARY?

A: The dead banks are the symbol of that time. So many banks expired through the national Default of 1998, and carried on after the same in a zombie way. There were too many of those. Why the Central Bank had not declared them bankrupt and let them siphon off their assets? Why the forward commitment to non-resident banks had been paid through the crisis? That is rather a rhetorical question. The Central Bank was involved with the same. Wealthy people were behind those banks.

The book series action starts back in 1998. The time of Default I keep close to my heart, I'm still living it through. They say, the time of troubles may come and go, while the people it touched still can't stop living it through. Why so? That maybe because life in Russia deserves the case name of Russian ennui that so many classics dwell on. At the time of Default it was done with, and there came the era of overindulgence and outlawry, that is to say, the times of freedom which had never more happened ever since. I am missing those days.

I: Tell me a little about your first thriller THE DEAD BANK DIARY.

A: This is the first novel from the series. You can read each novel independently. There are the same characters. My novels are not based on a true story – that would be stupid – but you will feel the reality. The story is told from the first person; it's me. No violent crimes, or anything of the kind. No politics or 'dangerous' Russian reality. Only MONEY. Beautiful financial schemes and frauds are in each novel. I love the beautiful gray area schemes on the verge of a crime. There will be a hostile takeover of a bank or forced bankruptcy. Raider attacks on banks attract me the most.

I: What attracts you to a bank raid?

A: I saw a bank takeover with my own eyes from the beginning to the end. This had an unsuccessful ending. But there was a moment when Victor said, *Imagine this is your own bank.*

Maybe Willie Sutton felt the same. It was no more pleasant than being in the bank at night alone.

I: Is there really a lot in your writing that has happened to you?

A: Yes, everyone in the stock market knew about it. Before default the banks fell down as a house of cards. Banks were pumped up with money and went bankrupt very easily. It was the period of wild capitalism, and I was lucky that time has passed through me.

I: You write you have been sick with millions...

A: Of course, big and easy money is like a drug. I hid this disease a long time, as alcoholics or addicts do. And then I used as well. Maybe I was lucky that I remained without work. I also realized that I would never get a job. What was important earlier to me lost its sense. I had a hungry look.

At that time I was mixed up. People had lost their former life. It was easy to get acquainted with everyone: a minister, a diplomat, a vice-president of the bank... I felt that time was not so long. That crazy time would leave as fast as a river. It would take the big fish away. It would go down to the depths. Already that time has gone. That time you could catch a big fish with your bare hands. I have nothing to regret.

I: Are these frauds real?

A: Yes, they are true. But to accomplish this you need an insider in the bank. Better someone on the bank board. Or you must get a lot of money to fall down the bank.

I: Is money the main thing in your novels?

A: Yes: if you're wondering how to get money out from thin air, the smell of money, how to reverse off-balance money, how to break banks, then my novels are for you. I write all about the money. The reader will always know what to expect.

I: The main hero of the series is Victor; meanwhile the hero of the first novel is Ilya. Why so?

A: Books are written in memory of Victor, a retired Foreign Intelligence Service officer and a fraudster. I was lucky to meet him. He died more than ten years ago. At the heart of all the novels will be my memories of him.

The hero of the first thriller and the following novels is Ilya, the bank's chairman. He is in his seventies. I imagine that some readers will be turned off by his age. But heroes come from anywhere. Writers sometimes say that characters find themselves. Ilya is a real person. He had become a hero unexpectedly for me. But I cannot tell who this character really is. In any case, all the heroes I've written about are real people. Default time in 1998 has made its own characters. They have been called the children of default. In real life they look like characters in a novel. It seems to me that the real life is much more interesting than any fiction.

I: Your novels are realistic, aren't they?
A: Exactly. While I worked as a market middleman, I made some digital recordings. That's a lot of hours of negotiations. I did not make these recordings for my

safety. There is no danger if you know the rules of Russian deals. Did I feel that very sharply at the time? I realized that the time of default would pass away. And to build a business from scratch would be impossible. I felt everything would come to an end very quickly. There were crazy days. I do not know why I've made these recordings. It was done by intuition. My novels have begun from these records. Some conversations were so interesting that they were included in the text with a few changes.

But the novels are not realistic. They are not like 'Liar's Poker' by Michael Lewis, for example. My thrillers are completely in line with the laws of the novelistic genre. Here there is intrigue, the heroes find out something unexpected about themselves, and there is a twist in the end. That is why in the first thriller I have got a US Federal Reserve Bond, face value one million dollars, issued in 1934. A very beautiful fake.

I: Was this bond real?

A: Oh, yes. Some fakes arrived on the market from various backgrounds. One of the most plausible stories says that a box with these bonds was taken out from Germany at the end of World War II. Boxes are gone around the world. So the Fed decided to devalue them. Dresdner bank issued a letter about its ability to accept the bonds. There was one thing: each bond had to have the Treasury Certificate, Global Immunity and Gold Bullion Certificate. But there were not. It's just a beautiful story. They say also that one of boxes taken out from Germany had been opened by one of our drunk generals. But it is known that some the European banks accepted these bonds as a deposit. I haven't held this bond in my hands. I had only a high-quality digital copy. It's a terrific document. And I have seen the parent papers. The stories about these bonds are so various... I told a one in my novel.

In fact, the story of a document from Dresdner Bank seems true. Once a casual acquaintance from special service said that not so many years ago, he unloaded trucks with trophies from German museums, which were brought from Moscow to Tomsk. There were leather-bound folios with engravings. They have not been packed and were unloaded without inventory. They were frozen in the thirty-degree frost.

I: Do you have any acquaintances from special service?

A: Just a few. These are the people from whom I try to be as distant as possible. But time goes on, things change. If someone said that I was seeking an 80-year-old professor, former officer of the NKVD (the People's Commissariat of Internal Affairs, the forerunner of the KGB), and we would have absolutely similar views on life, I would never believe it.

I: Is he Ilya?

A: Partly. Outwardly of course. He was a handsome, 6'5 feet tall, accustomed to getting any woman he wants.

I: And so your hero is in his seventies...

A: Yes, Ilya would not be the chairman of the bank if he was younger. It would be not plausible. But he is a strong hero. He loves risk. Do not worry, the main hero never will die and will not be ill at all. And what the hell can I do if this hero appeared, living his own life? He is stronger than me.

I: Your novels are written from the first person. You are the storyteller and the hero. How much truth is in your words?

A: Not a lot. But I am the reliable storyteller. You can trust me. There are two main heroes: Ilya and me. There is a main hero in two characters. I am the hero who could not pull off the plot. I am the type of hero who is called 'a magnet for shit'.

And Ilya, on the other hand, is the bastard. He breaks all the rules. He cannot be understood. He is not cruel himself. He has his logic. To be with Ilya is like making a deal with a devil. He doesn't need a victory or money. For him there is neither good nor evil. He simply stretches a hand and undresses who he needs. He can undress FSB (former KGB) or the church. He does not care.

Ilya is an outstanding character. I am glad that this hero has found me, and let me to write first four novels, and I hope there will be new one. He is inexhaustible. It's not just a thriller but a love story.

I: Tell me about yourself as a hero.

A: I'm a free trader, without any work, without a family and without any attachments. I've got a father. We met each other when I was a child, and I am happy with him. My heroes have also no family. They have a past, but I do not describe it. They simply live day by day. Each novel is one month in the lives of the characters. A story begins wherever it catches them. There are no memories.

I go on my way following the big money. It attracts me. I am infected with crazy millions. The people like me are few. Time has changed. It seems my kind doesn't exist anymore. I have an outgoing nature. But I love going after millions. It seems I will die on the run. I think I'm going mad. Where will I be on my way? Let me.

I: Are all of you heroes swindlers?
A: Yes, they are ordinary people. There are no good guys. There are no murderers. Losers just stay without money. Money is the most humane weapon.

I: Why are they so?
A: I have the answer in my second novel FOR

THOSE IN THE SHADE. They are that way by nature. They just eat each other. Sometimes literally. And there is nothing to do about it. It is simply a life. There is a beautiful and convincing psychological theory about it. It's founder is a Russian prof. Porshnev.

I: You have a philosophical degree. Are there other philosophical theories?

A: Nietzsche and Russian philosopher Berdyaev are closer to me. But in my novels there are no long conversations. My heroes do not sit down with a cup of coffee. Each novel has a theme and a counter-theme. For example, the person is against the tyranny of absolute power, or against the law of necessity.

I: How about you? Are you a badass hero?

A: Of course. But I found it hard to write about myself as a badass. It was real hell. Good guys seem boring and unrealistic to me.

I: How much do you write about Moscow?

A: Not a lot. It's so funny to see how Hollywood films

present Moscow as a dangerous city. Moscow does not differ from a European megalopolis.

But of course it is Moscow. I write about that time when the city was flooded with fantastic money. All was on sale: oil, gas, diamonds, public debts… The city breathed big money. I often write about it.

That time has gone, and the city was paralyzed without money. During that time empty buses were passing through downtown. And again Moscow began to choke with million-strong oil contracts, federal programs and cheap bank guarantees. Also there were offers of high yield private placement programs with sonorous names of the Top 100 European banks. With mad percentages. They had nostalgia for those days that had recently fallen. They smelled of the quiet life.

I: Don't you think Moscow is a dangerous city?
A: I understand your question. Well, as dangerous as an arms dealer? Maybe now there is some interest in Moscow, but I would not like to write more about Moscow as a landscape. Of course, my main hero has a bodyguard.

Is Russia dangerous? No. People with ideology are dangerous. Rich Russians have not got it. Ideology is for the poor. The poor cannot make a rich state.

I: Have you had a hard life? Are you writing much about yourself?

A: Not much. But I try to explain what a person feels after he has been gobbled up by a city such as Moscow.

Interview with Anna Schlegel, Author of FOR THOSE IN THE SHADE

I: Why did you choose this name of your thriller?

A: Once, my friend Igor, the retired intelligence officer, had heard at a meeting how someone gave a toast: FOR THOSE IN THE SHADE! He looked back and saw how the people whom he would never suspect as close to the Intelligence Service were reacting to this toast.

I: Are your heroes from the Intelligence Service?

A: Yes, but I do not write about it. The series of novels are based on my memories of a real person, Victor, a retired Foreign Intelligence Service officer. The time came that officers of the Foreign Intelligence Service held the post of vice president in the bank overnight. They had to forget about their lives as spies, and become bankers. A lot of them couldn't do this. They understood nothing about finances. To see them in banks was funny. Gone are the days of espionage, blackmail and other things they used to do.

To name Victor a financial fraudster would be more precise. Along with many others officers, he lost his connections with the Foreign Intelligence Service, once those who from the Intelligence Service felt lost themselves.

In the time of the Soviet Union, Victor had been living in Europe, working in European banks. He knew how the European bank system worked. This was possible only for Intelligence Service officers.

I: Why don't you write about the Intelligence Service?

A: I don't write what I don't know.

I: You say that you write about golden age of bankers, from 1998. What was special about those years?

A: In that time there was freedom. There was neither the police nor the intelligence services, or any crimes haven't prevent the banks to make money. The bank board was rather independent. Now the chairman of the bank is more often the hired manager with a big salary. Now there is no such freedom. Banks are rigidly subordinated to the Central Bank and their owners, the largest corporations. There are no more beautiful financial gray schemes, as they were in those days.

I: Have you come across crime?

A: No. Maybe you have heard about Russia's crime. But where the financiers were there was not crime. Banks were supervised by the Special Services and that's why there was not crime. It was something akin to the redistribution of spheres of influence. Where pure money turned out in financial schemes, there was not crime.

By the time of Yeltsin's decree in February 1996, the Foreign Intelligence Service was pumped up by money and officers came to the banks. The Intelligence Service began to be engaged in financial espionage. Also they began to gain power.

As to crime... Once I met a woman who had

diamonds with an estimated value of 125 million dollars. She had received this jewelry, which was named 'garbage collection', from the appraiser of jewels. The appraiser had been connected with criminal authority Michailov, aka Mikhas. Before meeting her I thought that only a man who put on a white shirt and tie every day could commit such a fraud.

Now Russian crime has changed. Children of fathers who killed for primary capital become polite managers and lawyers. The same as in America.

I: Does a financial fraud also take place in the plot?
A: Yes, one of the most interesting frauds.

I: About which financial frauds do you write? Are they real?
A: Sort of. I do not write about high-profile scams. The repayment of public debt was the most beautiful fraud of 1998. A very beautiful scheme. But it has been written about. There was one more beautiful transaction. It was made by the Russian immigrant

Arcady Gaydamak. It was named Angola gate. It has also been written about. And everyone knows about the Russian scandal with the Bank of New York. The IMF loan was transacted on foreign corresponding accounts. Those banks would have to transfer back rubles. But they paid it off with government bonds that were simply junk. The banks that made these transactions went bankrupt one by one, merging money through the BONY.

I write about frauds that can happen in a small bank. Such banks are called 'pocket banks'. They serve the accounts of one rich client who owns the bank. Raiders attack the bank, bankrupting and withdrawing money from the bank, pumping up the bank with money, money laundering... Really, no one robs banks better than the bankers. It is the so-called 'grey schemes'. Catching someone redhanded is very hard. Therefore in my novels there are no investigators or any investigations. Simply the big fish eats the small.

I: Are your swindlers unpunished?

A: Absolutely. To make a deal with G-men would just be silly. If someone falls into the hands of the State, he would not be convicted. To make an agreement is always possible. These are the rules of Russian game.

I: You say that your dialogue is realistic, and some things have been written down directly from digital records. In this novel as well?

A: Yes. The conversation with the owner of an airline in Guinea was included in the text just as it was on the recording. By the way, it was a woman who said it. She tried to deliver the aircraft in… no, not in Guinea.

I: FOR THOSE IN THE SHADE is your second thriller. Tell me a little about it.

A: Here are the same heroes, the same problems. But I think this novel is considerably different.

I: What is special in the thriller FOR THOSE IN THE SHADE?

A: I'm staying with Ilya. He is in his seventies. Between us is about thirty years. All the time I wonder why are we together? One day I met a friend of Ilya. He was not at all like Ilya. Still, they had a lot in common. We talk, drink vodka, go to Israel, and I understand everything that is happening to me. I understand what is holding me to Ilya. I do not believe in love without any reasons. I write this just as a hint, but it's a terrible allusion.

To say that it is fiction would not be true. It is my interpretation of an interesting psychological theory. In this way it is the truth. This theory can explain a lot. It was written at the beginning of the century by Prof. Porshnev. This theory is about human origins. The first people ate their fellow tribesmen. Animals ran away from them quickly. I think everyone knows about it. It is assumed that their descendants live among us. Imperceptibly. They are more cruel, more arrogant, and imperious, and all of this. This theory asks the question: Why are we so different?

You will feel the truth of this theory after reading FOR THOSE IN THE SHADE, and you will look at people a little bit differently. I promise.

You may also be interested in novels by Anna Schlegel

THE DEAD BANK DIARY SERIES

THE DEAD BANK DIARY

Book One of The Dead Bank Diary Series

ISBN: 9780986174919
ASIN: B00OPAZQMI

THE PRINTS ON THE SNOWS OF YESTERYEAR

Book Three of The Dead Bank Diary Series

ISBN: 9780986174988
ASIN: B017KYY2MA

SOME DAY I`LL HIT A BANK

Book Four of The Dead Bank Diary Series

ISBN: 9780998185323

THE FROZEN DEBT

Book Five of The Dead Bank Diary Series

ISBN: 9780998185309

MY GOD IS MONEY

Book Six of The Dead Bank Diary Series

Coming Soon

THE DEAD BANK DIARY

Book One of The Dead Bank Diary Series

by Anna Schlegel

ISBN: 9780986174919
ASIN: B00OPAZQMI

The rats living on the refuse of the bank backyard
stay full at all time

This is not a robbery. A bank is taken with all its guts: accounts, debts, points of exchange, the staff to the last secretary, the building. This is beautiful and clean fraud.

I was out of work, while all around you could smell millions, even in the air outside. It was an unforgettable smell of public debt, oilfields, gold, bank guarantees, diamonds... I wanted to breathe in the air of easy cash Moscow, to revel and roll in this air. I could feel the smell of money in the wind on my face. This air was used to make up funds overnight, to make a fortune, to go rack and ruin and then grow rich again. It was going free across the wreckage of the sold out Soviet empire.

I was asked to help redeem the debts of a bank. The insider man at the bank held the post of Vice President.

A bit of danger and a bit of love.

THE PRINTS ON THE SNOWS OF YESTERYEAR

Book Three of The Dead Bank Diary Series

by Anna Schlegel

ISBN: 9780986174988
ASIN: B017KYY2MA

The best to rob the bank is the banker himself

The Bank, facing bankruptcy, fell out of the hands like a snowball rolling downhill to flatten everything under its weight.

Behind every bankruptcy there are people who make it happen. But there are no influential people. Big figures are absent. It seems you stay face to face with the emptiness.

This happens when the Central Bank is playing against you.

SOME DAY I`LL HIT A BANK

Book Four of The Dead Bank Diary Series

by Anna Schlegel

ISBN: 9780998185323

The bomb lives to its internal time

My life became lonely and monotonous, almost mechanical in nature, with a mechanism akin to a ticking bomb. It could be ticking for days and weeks, quiet and imperceptible, to blow up everything around at the right time.

This way common folks used to live in the past, bakers and shoemakers. They lived their lives until the revolution burst out. It was their time. And then they went out the door of their bakery and shoe shop for good to take the ministry chairs and cut the heads off the aristocracy, by weaving plots and intrigues. I knew I will not miss my time.

It seemed to me I could go on for another ten years, and one day stumble on a terse line in the newspaper and realize: my time has come.

THE FROZEN DEBT

Book Five of The Dead Bank Diary Series

by Anna Schlegel

ISBN: 9780998185309

When totally nude have a look, maybe you still got the shoulder loops

One morning he stayed bare-ass, there was no money, no name, no wife, and nothing left... just his shoulder loops.

MY GOD IS MONEY

Book Six of The Dead Bank Diary Series

by Anna Schlegel

Coming Soon

---

*A bank is like a condom, you can only use one at a
time*

The rats are perennial, they'll exist till the end of times, wealthy and miserable, in the wild or in prison, through any shift in power or regime change, be that capitalism or communism, and nothing would ever alter them as they could adapt for any environment and their world of invisible omnipresence is well protected by their God, and no one would get out of His hand since their God is money.

SPY & FINANCIAL THRILLER

THE SLEEPER SERIES

MONEY CAN`T LIE

Book One of The Sleeper Series

ISBN: 9780998185330

ON MYSELF FOR LITTLE MONEY

Book Two of The Sleeper Series

Coming Soon

AUTHOR'S NOTE

There are no agents and no offices furnished with the electronics, it is free of everlasting arguments with the management and those talks of the crummy salaries.

He's an agent with no support, and he's got nothing on his hands... But then why, if he is a respectable banker in a European bank?

ABOUT THE SLEEPER SERIES

These are the books about someone I met in Berlin, and four days later I had to become his wife and his backer-up, the second key to the deal, the duplicate. It would not have happened if he had not turned into a transient target for the secret services, a mere bargaining chip. He was sold out as a long sleeping Russian agent.

The deal to which Vlad was a shadow partner was tied up.

This deal was about the discharge of foreign debts of several countries in Africa via a number of embassies and ministries, oil companies and stock trading businesses, through the German and Swiss banks... It involved over a hundred different partners, functionaries and security officials, company leads and multiple agents. And they were all hidden behind a bunch of middlemen. This deal was made of personal contacts and handshakes, of non-committal talks and of pure air. Once materialized, the deal incorporated proper ironware and Swiss-clock precision.

Who would not wish to hold this kind of deal in their hands? They were so many. It could make a perfect channel for arms or diamond trafficking.

However the people were the main asset of that deal. So it took us a while to realize in the wrong hands it could play on one occasion only, and that would be to knock out just a single man.

If only we had known this, it would be clear there was no coincidence, there was no token money in that big a game, and every player was worth a lot. Seven digits were invested into this deal takeover, and should they fall onto us in a banking package it would have crushed us like a block of concrete.

That time we were not aware of this. Vlad and I were making time pass in an empty house in the suburbs of Berlin along with vodka and cakes, trying to figure out why the hell the British intelligence had started to look out for Vlad as a Jewish mom?

They say, nothing bands people better than fear, neither love nor hatred.

These novels are not based on actual events but you can still scent the reality in every word.

MONEY CAN`T LIE

Book One of The Sleeper Series

by Anna Schlegel

ISBN: 9780998185330

Should there be three pieces of crap this is of the British intelligence classic

One day there happened what may happen to a sleeping agent, he was burnt by the same intelligence he worked for. He expected to be arrested and suddenly realized all those things he felt overwhelming for the last week were nothing but seeming true.

And in reality it was all quite different, and he had to save not his neck but the operation to which he was a shadow partner.

This deal left no legible trace. It was just like a woman always staying with somebody else in her pursuit of money. It was made of thin air, of powerful links, of noncommittal talks and handshakes. In this deal every cent was lying in someone's hands. So not knowing the hand that handed this cent over to some other hands one could learn nothing at all, and the whole thing turned to be a number of bulging bubbles of virtual money that disappeared from bank accounts with a single keystroke. It became the reality pulling in to death.

So many people wanted to hold that deal in their hands.

Therefore he understood nothing would happen to him there, he could just walk out with no glance back since he knew so well all those counterparties involved in this operation, and these people could sense something went wrong from miles away and could read it by his walk, there was no need to warn them, they would scatter away on their own and hideaway like rats. And the deal would vanish alongside with them, flowing like sand between his fingers.

If someone wanted to hold down that deal nothing wrong could happen to him. He just had to walk into the street.

But then, what if he was mistaken?

ON MYSELF FOR LITTLE MONEY

Book Two of The Sleeper Series

by Anna Schlegel

Coming Soon

The British intelligence cannot compromise its integrity, it will adhere to its principles like in the old times of rock 'n 'roll. And it's damn good to look at it working... but then it's scary to see it work against yourself.

He was not worth a straw to the intelligence, a mere sleeper, a small coin. One day he felt behind his back there was someone else, someone a big shot of so high value they could not afford to lose him. Who could that be, a recent turncoat? He had no idea.

He could only see a trace of him barely-there, just a tip. And they were seeking to ward the trail off, not just by drawing it aside as now it appeared leading straight to him. So that everything would point to him. The trace would be lifeless, of beautiful classics and as much stone-dead.

ABOUT THE AUTHOR

I was born in Moscow. I studied at the Moscow State University at the Philosophical faculty. I got a PhD in philosophy and stayed without work and without money. The financial crisis began. Some years I was looking for a work, but took it easy. I was a securities trader in an investment company by chance. And then there was the default in 1998. I was without work again.

This was my best time. I became the financial middleman of off-market private transactions. I had nothing. I have been looking for too-big deals. But then there was a time that it was quite possible for me to be the middleman in the sale of a Libyan oil tanker or the sale of aircrafts abroad. I got sick of conducting multi-million dollar transactions and lost all sense of reality.

I met Victor. He was a retired Foreign Intelligence Service officer. He was a magnificent fraudster. I understand how strange it sounds. But at that time before the Yeltsin decree in February 1996 the Intelligence Service was pumped up by money. And Intelligence Service officers one by one began to hold the post of deputy chairmen of the bank. It had happened overnight. Certainly, I could say: he was a magnificent financier, but... to call him as a financial fraudster would be more truthful.

Capturing the bank was in my sights. The insider of the bank was the vice-president of the bank. I write about his capture almost unchanged. Victor would be recognized by his conversations. Before leaving, he left me his three passports... So I do not know his real name. There were no closed doors for him. He had friends from the federal agency for government communication and information and from the board of directors of Deutsche Bank. All kinds of people.

Years passed. Victor is long gone. And there are fewer middlemen.

I feel myself to be on the way out. The whole generation is on the way out as well, those who are described as robbing the country.

I like those who robbed the country, and I'm

pleased how it was done. They were really talented financiers, nothing worse than financiers on Wall Street. They left the country and have taken the money with them.

Since then, Moscow's air did not smell of millions any longer. But it seemed to me, it was still in the depths of my house between a pile of white shirts.

Now there are no more financial middlemen. The young have got jobs first. They receive a salary at the end of the month, and seem to have already forgotten the smell of crazy millions. It's like being drunk. There's a dizziness from it... They did not want to breathe this air. They did not want to poison their lives. They earned their money. They had wives, children, dogs, cars, which it is necessary to care of... Their heads have been overflowing with thoughts of petty cash.

Then the middlemen were old. And I stayed with them. Therefore, the heroes of my novels are in their sixties.

For the former friends who stayed in the stock market I became infected. No, I just died. And I have been smelling of sweet cadaveric decay.

It seemed to me that I was among the dead. And it felt really bad for me as a living being. But I shared their way of thinking. I was the same as they were. Ridiculous and old-fashioned, useless clutter, rubbish. Market garbage.

My friends were precisely the same as a middle-aged gentleman.

Sometimes I catch a strange look at myself, but then forgot about it. The metropolis cleaned me from their memory. There was no need to be as nice as kind people who talk with clients and colleagues daily. I had a different way of talking. My talking always led to a deal. And in case it didn't, I would give the finger and immediately forget the useless person as if shaking off dust. And that's all.

I have nothing to regret. I had nothing to blame myself for. Dogs wouldn't blame themselves for their dog's life, would they?

I could not return back to the stock market. It has changed. Brokers, buyers, and sellers have been changed. They all had grown up a little. They have got each other for 0.1 percent interest, ready to set their ass to everyone at 0.5 percent, and would sell their own mother at one percent. I could not do that. The market has kicked me out as garbage.

And the old, among whom I used to be, are gone. The reality of small money has burnt out people around me as fire burns wood. Sometimes it seems to me that I have gone mad, that I live in the world turned inside out. Sometimes I would like to be like anyone… to have a rest, eat, dress, buy a car…

But I can't do it. It would be a living death.

It seems to me I would lose days and years and end up in devastation and poverty. And I would lose the scent of money, and the skill … I clung to the sale of oil, diamonds, and bank guarantees, though I'm sure that it was simply thin air and there was nothing behind it. Sometimes I woke up and thought that all was not with me. But I lived and breathed the air of millions. It was my life. In my life I gained money from thin air. Emptiness is a magnet for me.

Now I have got nothing. I do not care. I like my life. I like to go for millions. It's impossible to stop me. I might be put down like a mad dog.

And I still have a sense of money. I can smell

the street's air and say that the market has changed. It smells as sharp as the smell of fresh bread from a bakery in the frost.

FINANCIAL THRILLER

THE DEAD BANK DIARY

SERIES

THE PRINTS ON THE

SNOWS OF

YESTERYEAR

By Anna Schlegel

BOOK THREE

The best to rob the bank is the banker himself

CHAPTER ONE

THE BANKRUPT

Moscow, November 1999

Peter came back early. He came to the house and stayed on the doorstep. He smelled of snow, his sparse yellow teeth carried a smoldering cigarette. He did not take off his coat yet, the snow melting on his grey sprouted frizz, sticking to his wrinkled forehead. His soft and watery loose face seemed frozen.

"What happen, Peter?" I asked, shaking off the snow flakes from his coat collar, and taking the cigarette from his teeth for a pull.

"Ilya went bankrupt... By and by... rack and ruin..." he replied, looking away and picking out his cigarette from my suddenly stiffened fingers.

I had not expected this.

Ilya's bank was not making the top two hundred. It was what you call a pocket bank, formerly at the disposal of a major government company. Ilya became its chairman at first, in a nominal way. But over time the company left government custody, pulled its funds abroad, and the bank had eventually become Ilya's. He was running his business invisibly, for the most part, in Europe. He never intended to set it on any better path, and was keeping himself in shade.

However, this time Ilya had got it wrong. Peter and I, we had unwittingly stirred him to this.

It was a matter of a year and a half back, when Peter took the position of deputy chairman in Ilya's bank, and tried to take over the bank. I had slightly helped Peter. Ilya's bank was heavily in arrears and could hardly stay afloat; it appeared it hadn't been so difficult to get a hold of it. It seemed with just a bit more effort Ilya's bank would be in our hands. But Ilya managed to pledge Foreign Currency Bonds with some small European banks. Deutsche Bank issued him the bank guarantee against the bank securities of those hundred banks, so Ilya's bank received so much money it was impossible to approach.

But today those Foreign Currency Bonds had lost their value.

Our bank takeover had failed that time, but it had changed our lives. Peter's reputation was badly tarnished, and no bank would ever employ him. It was a shame since he actually was a born financier with a bulldog attitude. I had been jobless for a long time. Sometime in the past I used to be a trader in Securities, and resigned to run after multi-million-dollar business, until Peter picked me up like a stray cat, in my beaten up shoes with a hungry look.

Peter became just like me: a middleman in off-exchange trade. This kind of broker was considered the garbage of the market. We used to snatch at everything and anything without regard like two famished mongrels throwing themselves onto the bones left by the kitchen midden. They say buffalos would die of hunger and the hyenas would eat each other. No, this did not happen to us. Peter and I were hanging together like two bloaters, and the stronger the grip the less hope there was to get out of the shithouse, and we kept drowning there. Was it the misery holding us together? What could one earn in a dead market?

I had started looking at my reflection in the mirror more often lately, with attention and distance, examining my insipid and sharp face. Did it show I was moneyless? In the past, when I had an entire week of no transactions I was actually scared the sound of my voice would give me away, and it was clearly so. I actually used to notice it myself with the brokers I spoke with daily on the phone. I had a good antenna for money. The broker who can't make a deal makes people scatter as if he's a leper. And how much effort is required to hide the matter! So what will happen in a month time? I must have been wearing a – *No cash available, No cash...* – message across my forehead... I was looking at my reflection with the only thought, *Where can I hide that dead beat look?*

Peter and me, we were renting a two-room flat in the suburbs of Moscow, waiting for a chance to launch a raid on some other bank. This flat served us as a broker's office with a sole trader. There was nothing to hope for, however. Every morning, all week long except weekends, I was making porridge for Peter; we had breakfast together and parted to have our various appointments, and in the evening after dinner, we used to smoke thinking of what we could do the following day, and then each of us went to their bedroom.

On weekends I left for Ilya's house in the countryside. Sometimes Ilya sent a car for me midweek, and I joined him in his apartment. I had no business with Ilya. I just shared a bed with him.

Ilya was seventy, but neither he nor I, nor anyone else who used to know him would ever sense his age. In the market they used to say, Ilya had buried four of his deputies, and just caught a cold himself.

I could not refuse my meetups with Ilya and did not want to get any closer to him either. There were too many reasons. Ilya had been by himself all along. I did not want to be a burden for him. For a long time I had a feeling of Ilya's being tired, and too tired to kick me aside. But then I realized he found me easy to be with. Me and Peter, we used to get into all kind of crap, and I wouldn't wish Ilya to get into the same. I equally did not want Ilya to think of what I had stepped into. He had an entire shithouse to himself, actually. So he did not worry about me, as if he wanted me to have that crap to my heart's content. In the post-crisis stock-market there was enough of that crap to go around.

Initially it seemed to me that Ilya and me, we were far too different people. But nope, we were similar, as if as they say, we used to piss in the same pot as kids. I must have inherited my father's old-fashioned manners. Ilya used to tell me he could not shake the feeling he was speaking to me like to my father.

My father once told me, wincing as if he had a sore mouth, that he would be happy to talk to Ilya late in life, sitting in the diapers on a bench...

In a prison-yard, I used to joke.

In fact it was too late to change things. Ilya said, *We are late, baby.*

I was leading my own way, and Ilya was going his.

Who would have known the Foreign Currency Bonds would lose their value?

There was a collapse.

No one expected it to happen. The major Russian banks used to take out loans secured by government stocks, Foreign Currency Bonds, Eurobonds and obligations to the London Club. All of these had depreciated in a blink, to a mere ten percent of their face value. Our banks were, in a minute, losing hundreds of million dollars with this collapse. And the European banks concurrently called for additional payment of these stock values that were marked to the market and depreciating.

Eventually, Ilya lost over two hundred million dollars.

So he just did not have any funds. And he could not have any. His bank had no working capital at all.

Deutsche Bank, having realized it, with no chance of winning a lawsuit, took a decision to assign the right to recover Ilya's debt to another Russian bank, namely F-Group, and proposed Ilya take a merger with that bank.

Ilya did his best playing for time with his bank failure. His salvage for a while was in the moratorium on payments to non-resident banks. Still he had no chance to escape bankruptcy.

In the sober light of day, none of Ilya's key creditors, who were five small-scale defense industry enterprises, had no intention to drive him to bankruptcy. Ilya gathered his creditors and they took a decision to discard the bankruptcy, and signed for an amicable settlement with the bank. But this solution could satisfy neither Deutsche Bank nor the Central Bank.

Ilya himself had never enjoyed good relationship with the Central Bank. But F-Group bank, to whom Deutsche Bank was ready to assign the right to recover the debt, actually had rather good relationship with the Central Bank.

Basically, Ilya had to accept a merger with F-Group, who had already started making the paperwork ready.

"Have you seen Ilya?" I asked Peter, looking into his troubled face, where a flurry of thoughts seemed over-run by a ripple of wrinkles.

"Yeah. Ilya has appointed me vice-chairman in one of the banks. Not a bank actually, but a shithouse incidentally still holding its license."

"Why does Ilya need that bank then?"

"No idea. One of its shareholders has transferred the management of his parcel of shares to Ilya. The rest Ilya has taken as lien, real cheap. Who would refuse?"

"So what did Ilya say?"

"He told me to knock the bank into shape, told me to boost the charter capital. No problem. But I find it a shame to be even asking for money for such a bank. One is ashamed to ask people in, actually. It's a dog-hole office. I'm a horse's ass with my teeth missing. Who would be talking to me? I told Ilya, *Give me some cash to place a golden ashtray in the meeting room, at least.* And he wouldn't. He's got no cash!"

"Why this ashtray?" I did not get him.

"It's simple. A wealthy client comes to see a gilded ashtray. Then I take him to my friend's bank, there is a similar gilded ashtray. The client gets to think I have opened a branch office, and plunks down his money."

"Can you ever meet such dummies really?" I smiled.

"It's not hard work to place an ashtray... "

"What's this F-Group?" I snapped at Peter.

"I don't know. Why this particular F-Group? The Central Bank wanted it this way," Peter stretched out for a cigarette.

Having a smoke after Peter, I was thinking for the whole of my relationship with Ilya to be over. There was nothing out of the ordinary; I had been meeting Ilya at the porch of his country house. I could no longer do without these dates. And from now on, there seemed be no more of these. The bankruptcy would kill the little we had together. Everything around me appeared to be as fragile as glasswork. As if a glass incidentally flew out of my hands with all of its contents spilling, and smashed into smithereens.

A wave of hunger came to my throat, as it usually was when Ilya left.

"So how is Ilya himself?" I asked catching myself asking about Ilya as if I had not seen him a while, and had little chance of seeing again.

"Ilya is sinking, and dragging everyone with him. He's doing real bad. Everyone is scattering from him as if he were plague-stricken," Peter said in a softer tone, smoothing out his wrinkled forehead like ceasing crease marks on the water. "He wants to go Switzerland to speak to each of his creditors privately... And who would let him go to Switzerland with that much debt? His feet-first only."

Anna Schlegel has a degree in philosophy. She was Securities trader before the recession. The last ten years she has been involved in off-market private transactions as a middleman in Moscow.

Anna lives in Novi Sad, Serbia.

CONTACTS INFORMATION

For information about the author, please visit TheDeadBankDiary.com, thedeadbankdiary@gmail.com

For information about the published books, please contact Schlegel Press Association at schlegelpressassociation@gmail.com

Anna Schlegel

www.ingramcontent.com/pod-product-compliance
Lightning Source LLC
Chambersburg PA
CBHW070932130626

46555CB00001B/393